two songs

TWO SONGS BY OKOT p'BITEK
illustrated by Trixi Lerbs

song of prisoner

song of malaya

Heinemann Kenya

Published by
Heinemann Kenya Ltd.,
Kijabe Street,
P.O. Box 45314,
Nairobi.

First published in 1971
First published by Heinemann Kenya 1988

ISBN 9966 – 46 – 720 – 3

Printed by English Press Ltd.
Enterprise Road,
P.O. Box 30127, Nairobi, Kenya.

for Patrice Lumumba

song
of
prisoner

contents

1

dung of chicken

The stone floor
Lifts her powerful arms
In cold embrace
To welcome me
As I sit on her navel.

My head rests
On her flat
Whitewashed breasts.

She kisses
My bosom
My neck
My belly button
My back
My buttocks
And shoots freezing bullets
Through my bones.

That giant firefly
On the high ceiling
Rains fiery hailstones
Into my closed eyes
Punching holes
Through the thatch,
There is a colourless rainbow
On the bleak white walls
And on the brow
Of the weeping stone floor . . . .
        *   *   *
Do you plead
Guilty
Or
Not guilty?
        *   *   *
I plead drunkenness,
I am intoxicated

With anger,
My fury
Is white hot,
My brain is melting,
My throat
Is on fire.

I am dizzy
With frustration,
I am drowning
In the deep Lake
Of hatred,
My heart is riddled
With the arrows
Of despair,
My head is bursting . . . .
Oh!

    *   *   *

See the muscles
Of my arms,
I can break your neck,
Do you realise that?

Do you know
I was a footballer
And a boxer ?
I have been a wrestler

And a runner,
I am a great hunter,
I have killed three buffaloes
And a hippopotamus
Single-handed . . . .

    *   *   *

Look at the laughing wound
In my head
Its cracked negro lips
Painted with dirty brown ochre,
Do you see
The beads of blood
On my legs and feet?
My nose
Is a broken dam,
Youthful blood leaps
Like a cheetah
After a duiker,
Two fingers
The width of the new gap
In my teeth . . . .

    *   *   *

Brother,
How could I
So poor
Cold
Limping

Weak
Hungry like an empty tomb,
A young tree
Burnt out
By the fierce wild fire
Of Uhuru

How could I
Inspire you
To such heights
Of brutality?

Brother,
I am not a witch,
I was not caught
Dancing stark naked
Around your house,
Did you find me
In bed with your wife
Or raping your mother?

Why should I not
Sleep with the green grass
In the City Park
While I nurse
My hunger?
Why do they call me

A vagrant
A loiterer?

*   *   *

Your Honour,
Why do they beat me
With their clubs
And tie my hands
And feet
With this rope?
Why do they box
And slap me?
Why do they ram my feet
With the butt
Of their rifles?

Your Honour,
Why do they
Punish me
Before I plead
Or am found
Guilty?

*   *   *

The dark silence
Urinates fire
Into my wounds,
The hollow laughs
Of my uniformed Brothers

Fan the fire
I am engulfed
By a red whirlwind
Of pains
Hotter than the pangs
Of childbirth,
More deadly than
The venom
Of the black mamba . . . .
         *   *   *
My children howl
Like mad dogs,
A lullaby is stuck
In their mother's throat.
My father
Is asleep
In the stomach
Of the earth
Unseeing
Unhearing
Undreaming.

Listen to the footsteps
Of the wizard
Dancing on my father's
Grave.

*Listen to the Chief's dog
Barking like a volcano
Listen to the echoes
Playing on the hillsides!*

2

wounded crocodile

The foul smell
Of the world
Rises like cumulus clouds
And clings on the bare walls
Like a baby monkey
On its mother's back . . . .

My lungs hurl themselves
Against each other
Like boxers in the ring,

My heart shouts
Like the referee
And tries to separate them . . . .
        *   *   *
Listen to the Chief's dog
Barking like a volcano,
Listen to the echoes
Playing on the hillsides!
How many pounds
Of meat
Does this dog eat
In a day?
How much milk . . . ?
        *   *   *
Have you seen
The mosquito legs
Of my children?

A witch
Has sprayed yellow paint
On their heads,
Their infant pregnancies
Are years overdue. . . .

My wife cleans her pot,
Her kitchen fire
Burns gently,
The water simmers . . . .

She and her children
Sit and wait
For the beans
Maize flour
And salt
Which I promised
To take home
For lunch!

*   *   *

My children's heads
Are bowed down
With heavy sleep,
But their stomachs
Drum sleep off
Their eyes. . .!

*   *   *

I plead hunger
Fiercer than a
Wounded crocodile,
Olympic athletes throw javelins
Inside my belly.

A Saharan thirst
Engulfs me,
My tongue hangs out
And I pray to Lazarus,
        Brother Lazarus,

Please,
Just a drop...!

The cry of my children
And the sobs
Of my wife
Haunt me like
A vengeful ghost.

The fiery lips
Of my sister's song
Burn me like leprosy,
The hammer of my mother's
Helpless ululation
Bashes my brain ....

I plead insanity,
I am
Mad,
Can't you see?

        *   *   *

The owls
Keep silence,
Cocks refuse to crow,
Bats clap their wings
Against the black mud
Of the night
In which

The Eagle
Of Time
Is stuck!

And I
Trembling,
Hungry,
Mad,
Sit,
Spit,
Shit,
Hate,
Wait . . . .

I plead smallness . . .
I am an insect
Trapped between the toes
Of a bull elephant

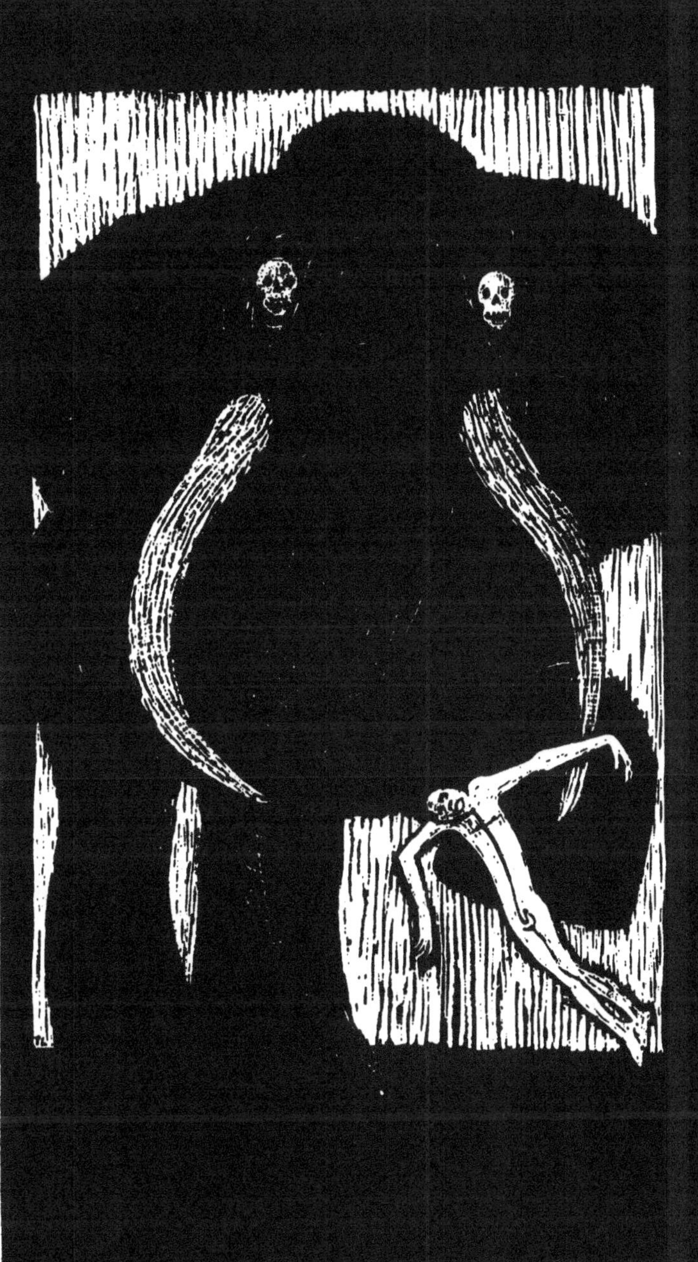

3

black mud

Listen to the drizzles
Dancing lightly
On the leaf of the
Olam trees,
Do you hear
The faint rhythms
Of their feet
And of their drums?

Listen to their
Mocking songs
Accompanied by the haughty horns
Of my Brothers' jeers . . . .

            *   *   *

Ten uniformed Stones
Break into my tiny hell,
Elephants trumpet
Rhinos scream
For blood
And charge,
The earth shakes her belly,
The walls jump
And dance,
The stone floor
Urinates
Orgasm . . . .

            *   *   *

Do you plead
Guilty
Or
Not guilty?

My mother slashes
The black sky
With her ululation,
My sister mumbles a dirge

And rolls herself
In the dust.

An alarm is raised
The war drum rumbles
Like thunder
Over the Lake,
War horns
Pierce the walls
Like bullets . . . .
My clansmen
Are gathered
The blades of their spears
And swords
Embrace the faint moonlight
And dance like butterflies
Over the corpse
Of a rat.

The warriors
Push the dark wind
With their buffalo-hide shields . . . .

     *   *   *

Old hyenas
Fight over the remains
Of a Lamb,
They suck

The eyeballs
And tear painlessly
At the tongue,
Penis,
Testicles . . . .
       *   *   *
A stone wall
Of guns
Surrounds our village,
Steel rhinoceroses
Ruin the crops
In the fields
And sneeze molten lead
Into the grass thatched huts,

Roaring kites
Split the sky
And excrete deadly dungs
On the heads
Of the people,
Pots and skulls
Crack . . . .
       *   *   *
Do you plead
Guilty
Or
Not guilty?

I plead smallness,
I am a mare
Pygmy
Before your
Uniformed Power
Which towers like
Mount Elgon
And covers the Land
With its dark shadow.

My ear drums
Are torn
I cannot hear you,
A red wall
Stands between you
And me,
I cannot see you,
But I feel
The cold blade
Of your axe
On my neck!

I plead fear,
I plead helplessness,
I plead hopelessness.

I am an insect
Trapped between the toes
Of a bull elephant,
I am an earthworm
I grovel in the mud,
I am the wet dung
Of a chicken
On the floor!

4

bon fire

The setting sun
Pours blazing oil
Into the Lake,
The water is covered
With the blood
Of dying hippos,
Crocodiles, fish
And fishermen . . . .

*   *   *

You
My old man
Rotting in the earth,
What an idiot
You were!

Why did you choose
This stupid bitch
For a wife?

Why did you vote
For this silly girl
To be my mother?

You should have known
The Clan
In which the most intelligent
Hardworking,
Thrifty
Ruthless
And most successful Chiefs
Are born and bred....!

Father,
But you were handsome,
Your limbs were powerful,
You were a great dancer!
I inherited my drumming talents

From you,
Did I not?

Why did you
Not elope with a girl
From the right Clan?
Why did you not woo her
With your colourful headgear
And the songs of the 'mother drum'?,
Could you not rape
A woman from the
Right Clan
And make her pregnant?

Why did you
Not scatter your seeds
In the air
So that the wind may
Plant them in the rich
Black soil of the great
Clan?

Do you not know
That offspring inherit
Intelligence,
Hard work,
Thrift,
Ruthlessness
And success

From their mothers?

*   *   *

Listen
You fool,
When I get out
Of this hell,
I will exhume your bones
And hang you
By the neck . . . .

I will kick
Your stupid skull
And punish you
For the sins
Of your boyhood days.

I will look
For the grave of
Your father
And dig him up,
I will discover
The grave of your mother
And dig her up.

I will make a big
Bon fire
And burn your bones
To ashes . . .!

5

sacred rock

The stone floor
Weeps ice tears,
Poisoned thorns
Pierce my naked feet,
The sweating walls
Shoot needles
Into my back
And throw cold insults
At me.

*My feet are a pair
Of pregnant women
Heavy like grinding stones . . .
My penis
Is an elephant's trunk*

The heavy smell
Of Death
Fills the room
Like darkness,
The alcohol
Of the black silence
Intoxicates me.

There is a carpenter
Inside my head,
He knocks nails
Into my skull.

My feet are a pair
Of pregnant women
Heavy like grinding stones
And full of the fangs
Of the cobra . . . .

My penis
Is an elephant's trunk
Vomiting blood
Like a woman
In her moon,
My wife is
The barusus palm
That has fallen
On a dung heap,

Her breasts heave
And whisper a welcome,
She is cold,
She sobs,
Her body rocks
With grief and regrets.

My bed
Is a Lake
Of tears . . . .

    *   *   *

A black Benz
Slithers smoothly
Through the black night
Like the water snake
Into the Nile,
Listen to it purring
Like a hopeful leopard,
Listen to its
Love song,
The soft poem
That embraces the valleys
And caresses the hills . . . .

The grasses on
The pathway
Hiss in protest,
The shrubs scratch

Its ribs
With their nails,
Foxes hit the windscreens
With their laughter,
Dogs whine
And sharpen their teeth,
The gods riddle the car
With yellow arrows
Of starlight . . . .

  * * *

My bed yells
In rhythm,
Woman giggles
And shrieks
In sweet agony . . .

Man breathes heavily,
Bathes in sticky sweat
And hides his shameless face
Between the large breasts
Of my woman . . . .

Big chief
Is dancing my wife
And cracking
My sacred rock!

  * * *

Do you plead

Guilty
Or
Not guilty?

*   *   *

I plead
Guilty
To hatred,
My anger explodes
Like a grenade,
And destroys like a hurricane,
My jealousy is darker
Than the coming storm
And madder than thunder . . . .
Cut off this rope,
Free my hands and feet,
I want to chase
The thief,
I will smell him out
And smear the road
With his brain . . . .

He throws sacks
Of dust
Into my eyes
And deluges me
With a bucket
Of mud,

His spittle covers me
Like dew
And makes me stink
Like gonorrhoea
He wipes his arse
On my head
And plucks off
All my feathers,
He throws me into a pond,
I shiver
My teeth clatter
While he nestles on the bosom
Of my young wife . . . .

      *   *   *

I want to drink
Human blood
To cool my heart,
I want to eat
Human liver
To quench my boiling thirst,
I want to smear
Human fat on my belly
And on my forehead.

Mix chyme
With goat blood
And I will drink it,

My inside is full of fire
I must drink
Human blood
To cool me down . . . .

6

this stupid bitch

A bird's song
Breaks through the high ceiling,
It is the ladybird
Collecting nectar
From the banana blossom
And flying back
To her nest.

The chicks
Chip their thanks
In unison . . . .

        *   *   *

I plead sickness,
I am an orphan,
I am diseased with
All the giant
Diseases of Society,
Crippled by the cancer
Of Uhuru
Far worse than
The yaws of
Colonialism.
The walls of hopelessness
Surround me completely,
There are no windows
To let in the air
Of hope!

        *   *   *

Mother,
Mother,
Why did you choose
An ugly and ignorant fool
For a husband?

Why did you elect
This poor man
From the wrong Clan
To be my father?

50

Did you not know
The right Clan,
The ones that produce
The most beautiful,
Most powerful,
The cleverest
And most successful men?

Why were you
In such a rush
To get married,
Mother?

But you were beautiful,
Your voice is still smooth
And sweet
Like refined honey,
Could you not
Woo a man from
The right Clan
With your song?
Could you not entice him
With the twist
Of your soft waist
And lure him
With your oiled smile
Into the grass?
Could you not

Persuade and encourage him
With your mock refusals?
Mother,
Could you not bribe
Or blackmail
A man from the right Clan
To sleep with you
And make you pregnant?
Do you not know
That children inherit
Beauty,
Power,
Wealth,
Cleverness
And success
From their fathers?
Do you not understand
What heredity
Is?

                *   *   *

Listen to the song
Of the flies
Feasting on the eyesores
Of the blind beggar,
They call me
A foreign bastard,

They describe my clansmen
As fools and weaklings,
Can you hear them saying
That my Clan
Will never rise to Power,
And I will die in deep poverty
And my children
Will become thieves?

    *   *   *

Our children will play
And swim in the stream
And hook fish
For the afternoon meal . . . .

7

voice of a dove

The tiny **lagut** bird
Carries a leaf of grass
To the **olango** thorn bush
To erect a hut
For her children
Who knock loudly
At the gate
And scream
To be let out . . . . .

*   *   *

Wife
Wife,
Are you asleep already?
Is my son
Kissing your teats
In his sleep?

Sleep peacefully
My love,
Dream sweet dreams,
Dream about our first meeting
In the forest . . . .

When you hear
The great news
Jump with joy,
Take the battleaxe
From under the bed
And dance the war dance,
Cut the earth with the axe
And make ululations,
Rejoice, my love!

When you hear
I have been arrested
Do not waste
Your kindly tears

Not a sob
Not a shriek,

I will not be hanged,
I will plead
Not guilty,
The best lawyers
Will defend me,
Our black nationalist judges
And those who hired me
Will set me
Free . . . .

    *   *   *

A python enters
Into a dead termite mound
And swallows the edible rat
And all its young.
An ostrich races
Across the dry plain
To cover her eggs
As the storm threatens . . . .

    *   *   *

Wife,
Tell the children
Not to cry for me,
Let them be proud
Of me,

Teach them the war song
About me,
Let them sing it every day,
Let them learn to be proud
And brave
Like their father!

My love,
Sleep for the last time
In that old hut
With the leaking thatch,
Sleep for the last time
On that dirty papyrus mat
On the earth.
I have bought
A farm
In the fertile valley,
A thousand acres
Of heaven
For you and me
And our children.

The crested cranes
Dance love dances
By the stream
That flows gently
Through our garden,
Our children will play

And swim in the stream
And hook fish
For the afternoon meal ....
Your house stands
On the chest
Of a small hill ....
Darling,
Your bed is soft
Like the voice of a dove
And warm
Like the womb...!

The sharks of Uhuru
Devour their own children,
The heads
Of their blood brothers
Bash with the battle axes
Of their tails!

8

distant echoes

The **lek** lizard
Wields his **deadly tongue**
And smashes a mosquito
To death...
There are tears of joy
In his eyes!

The sharks of Uhuru
Devour their own children,

The heads
Of their blood brothers
Bash with the battle axes
Of their tails!

I hear
The triumphant song
Of the hero of Uhuru,
Listen to him
Shout his praise name,
Hear his footsteps
As he prances
The mock-fight
Of victory . . . .

     *   *   *

Yes
I did it
And,
My God,
What a beautiful
Shot!

     *   *   *

The crickets whistle
In   sorrow,
Young toads leap
In the air
And yell for help,

Mama frogs blow
Cold air
Into their burning throats
And croak their children
To bury their heads
Into the cold mud . . . .

*   *   *

I am not senseless,
I am not cowardly,
Not dastardly,
I am not a thug,
I am not insane,
This is not
Cold-blooded murder,
I did not do it
For the money . . . .

He was a traitor
A dictator
A murderer
A racist
A tribalist
A clannist
A brotherist . . .

He was corrupt
A reactionary

A revisionist
A fat black capitalist
An extortioner
An exploiter . . . .

* * *

A fat mosquito
Hums a sweet song
And soothes
The 'snoring sleeper . . . .

* * *

You uniformed Brothers
Beating me now,
Why do you not
Salute me?
Form a guard of honour
So that I may inspect you,
Let the band play
Heroic tunes
As you march past me,
Shout three cheers
And congratulate me . . . .
He was a spy
A dirty dog
Of foreign powers,
A puppet dancing
To the songs of

Imperialist masters,
His stony cruelty
Covered the Land
Like the black darkness
Of the night,
Men choked in silence
Their chests breaking
With unspoken opinions
And unexpressed feelings.

The jails are filled
With men and women
Chained to their beds
Like penned goats . . . .

 *   *   *

The **til** antelopes
Graze on the steep hillside,
The waters of
The swift river
Rush over rugged rocks,
Leaping like young athletes
And singing a new song
In praise of rain.

Two bulls wrestle
With their horns,
The horn of the ruling bull

Breaks
And he tumbles down
The smooth breast
Of the hill
And plunges
Into the river.

9

jubilant throng

A long convoy
Of black ants
Winds its way
Through the wilderness
Bearing their booty,
They return home
To feast . . . .
The queen mother
Of the hillock

Weeps alone. . . !

*   *   *

You young widow
In black,
How beautiful you are
With those beads of tears
Glittering on your cheeks,
How dignified
The bearing of your
Sorrow-ridden body!
Do not blame me
Sister,
Do not be angry with me,
Do not hate me
You true Daughter
Of the Land.

Your husband was
An obstacle blocking
The path of Our Progress,
He had to be urgently removed . . . .

I had to kill him,
And I did it kindly,
He did not suffer long,
He died instantly!

He was arrogant

And your beauty spurred him on,
His words were swords,
Heads rolled when he spoke . . . .

     *   *   *

When you embraced
Your man
In your soft bed,
Other wives wept alone
Covered only by the blanket
Of bitter agony,
And taunted by the memories
Of past embraces.

When you sat around
The table
And joked with him,
Other wives sang red dirges
And beckoned the ghosts
Of their murdered husbands.

When you heard his voice
Through the telephone
And saw him on television,
Others played with
The distant echoes
Of dead men's voices.

When you walked hand in hand

By the Lakeside
And let the starlight
Dance on your white teeth
As you smiled and giggled,
Other wives cut
The veins of their neck
To let their black sorrows
Flow with their blood!

    *   *   *

My sister,
Do not be angry with me,
Show gratitude to me,
I have done a great thing
I have liberated
The People
And have made you
Famous!

10

killer mark

Open this steel gate
You uniformed Brothers,
Open the door
And let me out.

Where's your nationalism?
Where is your patriotism?
Where is your love
For the Motherland?

Open the door,
I want to go home,
I want to be with my children,
I want to talk with my wife.
I do not want to hang
By the neck
Until I am cold
And dead.

I want to plough the land
And plant the millet,
The planting season
Will soon pass . . . .
            *   *   *
Cut off this rope
Free my hands and feet,
I want to go to the church
And receive holy communion,
Our black nationalistic bishop
Will bless me
With the holy water.

I want to go to the village
To perform
The cleansing ceremony,
To deaden the sharp spear
Of the vengeful ghost,
Let the elders gather

At the clan shrine,
Let them spear
A black billy goat
And pour its blood
On the village pathway,
I will step on the blood
And smear it on my feet
As I enter the homestead.

The women will wail
Their welcome,
My mother will spit blessing
On my forehead,
And the Elder
Will cut the killer mark
On my back...!

   *   *   *

I want to join
The jubilant throng
Gathered at the City Park
Waiting for me,
I want to receive
Their thunderous applause ....

I want to raise my hands
And acknowledge
Their cheers,
I want to shake hands

With the Saturday morning shoppers
And wave to motorists
And cyclists . . . .

Let the People see
The hero
Of Uhuru!

*   *   *

Let Parliamentarians
Rise and honour me,
Let them award me
The highest prize
In the Land,
Let musicians
Compose songs about me,
Let the Chiefs
Organise celebrations
Throughout the Country.

Let the People
Drink and dance,
Let them rejoice,
For
The corrupt dictator
Is dead,
The noose on their necks
Is cut . . . .

I have done
A great Deed
And have become
Immortal!

11

soft grass

Shhhhh!
Listen,
Listen to the millipede
Whispering a lullaby
To her newly hatched baby,

Do not make noises,
Do not disturb
The sleeping one!

    *   *   *

Stop it,
Stop it,
I am a Minister,
Do you not know me?

Do you not
Recognise my voice?
Have you not heard me
Addressing meetings
Or on the radio?
Have you not seen me
On television?
Have you not seen
My pictures in newspapers
And in books?

    *   *   *

An earthquake erupts,
The steel door threatens
To tear off and fall on me,
The roofs laugh scornfully
And the bleak white walls
Jeer and cheer . . . .
Don't touch me
With your dirty hands,
Don't touch me
With those rude clubs . . . .

Stop it,
Stop it . . . .

 * * *

I hear the brown ants
Shouting war cries
And blowing horns
As they throw back
The first line
Of termite warriors
In the bloody battle
Of the hillock . . . .

 * * *

I am responsible
For Law and Order,
I am responsible
For Peace and Goodwill
In the Land,
I am your minister
You are my officers,
I command you . . . .

 * * *

The yellow acacia thorn tree
Lifts up her arms,
Her clean fingers
Speak soft invitations
To the yellow birds,
One hundred of them

Are gathered . . . .

Listen to their bitter chorus,
The protests and curses,
I see them
Shake their heads
And spit with contempt . . . .

A young man hurls a stone,
The yellow birds
Scatter in all directions
Leaving one struggling
Uselessly for life,
Listen to the anger
In the song
Of their wings . . . .
                *   *   *
Where is my secretary?
Ring up my wife
And tell her
I am on safari
And will not come home
Tonight.

Tell her I will be back
In two or three days . . . .
I am sure
I will be free

Next week . . . .

   *   *   *

The Rhinos of Uhuru
Kiss their brothers
In the back,
A fountain of red water
Cools the parched earth
And the scorched leaves
Of grass . . . .

   *   *   *

Ring up my friend and clansman,
I want to speak to
The chief of the army,
Ring up all my Brothers
In the army and police,
I want to tell them
That my life
Is in danger,
That our Clan
Is in danger,
I want them to look
After my wife and children,
And to make plans . . . .

   *   *   *

The groans of a Bull
Pour like the waters
Of the Wang-kwar fall

And cover the Land
Like a flood!

*   *   *

Where is my gold pen?
I want to write letters
To my children
And send them money.

I will not tell them
I am here,
I don't want them
To know that I am
A prisoner,
I want them to grow up
Without suffering,
I want them to pass
Their examinations
And get good jobs
And buy land,
Houses,
Cars . . . .

I do not want my children
To get shocked,
I do not want them
To feel sad and sorry
And cry for me,
I do not want them to know

That my hands and feet
Are tied with ropes
And I am sitting
On the naked thigh
Of the stone floor . . . .

      *   *   *

There is an empty chair
In the cabinet room,
The occupant is on leave,
He is alone
Buried in soft cottonwool
Thoughts of hope
Filled with poisoned needles
Of hopelessness . . . .

      *   *   *

Where is my writing pad?
I want to write
To my parents,
I want to send a fat cheque
To my old mother
And another fat cheque
To my old father . . . .
But how can I tell them
That I am shoeless,
That my feet are swollen,
Blistered and bleeding?
How can I tell

My mother that I am
Naked and bruised
All over?

I do not want
My mother to kill herself,
I do not want
My father to die
Of a heart attack ....

I will tell them
That I am coming home
To see them
Very soon ....

12

youthful air

Big chiefs are gathered
At the Embassy,
They click glasses
And exchange winks
With glittering wives
And false smiles
With husbands . . . .
    *   *   *

Wake up
You pressmen of the world,
I want to speak to you,
For the candle
Of Uhuru
Has been blown out . . . .
What is Uhuru
When all my thoughts
Are deep and silent rivers
Blocked up by concrete walls
Of fear and black suspicions?

How can I think freely
When the very air
Has ears larger than
Those of the elephant
And keener than the bones
Of the ngege fish?

Why are the words I speak
Captured and locked up
In a safe?

Open this steel gate
And let me out.

I want to breathe the air
Of my own choice,

I want to wake up early
Before the morning birds
Begin to sing
And swim in the naked air
Of the dying night,
I want to walk
On the soft grass
Of the olet grazing ground
And share the sleepy air
With the cows and goats.

I want to sleep
With the sand
At the sea shore
And expose my belly
To the spears of the sun
And swallow the boiling air.

I want to inhale
The youthful air
By the Lakeside
And intoxicate my lungs
With its alcohol.

I want to cool my head
With the dew
Of the morning grass ....

Open this door

And let me out,
The darkness in here
Chokes me . . . .

  * * *

You waiter
Standing there with the tray,
Bring me a large whisky,
No ice, no water . . . .
I want to drink it clean,
I want to drink
A whole bottle of whisky
To quench my thirst
For freedom,
I want to drink
And get drunk . . . .

I want to drink
With my friends in the bar
And at the night club,
I want to sleep
With experienced prostitutes.

I want to drink
With the peasants
In the fields,
And with the old women
In my constituency,
I want to suck **lacoi beer**

And share the sucking tube
With the old men
Around the fire.

Let the French girl
Bring her sexy cognac
And I will drink it,
I will cover her
With my broken kisses.

Let the Munyoro girl
Bring her sickly **amarwa**
And I will share it with her,
I will touch her unbroken breasts.

I want to drink
The honey beer and **waragi**
And the apartheid wine
From South Africa,
Let the Russians bring
Their red vodka
And I will drink it
With my Chinese friends
And break the glasses
On the walls,

Let the Kikuyu
Brew the **njohi**
And mix it with blood,

I will drink it
And give some to
The gallant forest fighters . . . .

I want to drink
All the drinks
Of the world,
I want to meet
All the drunkards
And chat with them . . . .

I want to drink
And get drunk,
I do not want to know
That I am powerless
And helpless,
I do not want to remember anything.

I want to forget
That I am a lightless star,
A proud Eagle
Shot down
By the arrow
Of Uhuru!

*My children do
Not go to school . . . .
They will grow up
With the wild trees
Of the bush
And will be burnt down
By the wild fire
Of the droughts!*

13

cattle egret

My children gather stars
Into their soft songs
And woo the young moon
With their white teeth.

The moon kisses
My daughter's emerging breasts
And my son's dimples . . . .
  * * *

I plead guilty
To pride,
I was not born to this,
I am a great soul
My mother knows this
My uncle told me so
And my father was proud
Of me . . . .

My children call me
Papa!
They run to me
And fall into my arms,
They sing and dance for me
And play games with me.

      *   *   *

The testicle of the bell
Knocks hard against
His round thighs
And he screams in sharp pain.

Tired teachers wipe
The chalk dust
Off their faces,
The school dam bursts
And floods of hungry children
Melt into their mothers' bosoms.

100

My children are
Not among them,
My children do
Not go to school
My children will
Never go to school.

The teachers' cane
Will never touch
Their buttocks,
They will grow up
With the wild trees
Of the bush
And will be burnt down
By the wild fire
Of the droughts!

  * * *

The proud cattle egret
Flourishes his long
And colourful tail
And dances between his
Wives and chicks ....

  * * *

Look at my athletic thighs,
My chest was broad
And without a scar,
My teeth were the

White **okok** birds
Standing on the back
Of a buffalo bull . . . .

Have you heard me
Playing the mother drum?
Have you seen me
In the dancing arena?
Cut off this rope,
Free my hands and feet,
I want to clap my hands
And sing for my children
So that they may dance,
I want to drum the wall
With my hands,
I want to jump up
And dance . . . .

Let me beat the rhythm
Of the **orak** dance,
Let my wife shake
Her soft waist before me
And remind me of our first meeting
At the dancing arena . . . .
I want to join the youths
At the 'get-stuck dance'
I want to suck the stiff breasts
Of my wife's younger sister,

I want to wrestle
With my wife-in-law
And crush the young grass
Beyond the arena . . . .
    *   *   *
Is today not my father's
Funeral anniversary?

My clansmen and clanswomen
Are gathering in our village,
They sit in circles
In the shades of granaries,
But who will make
The welcome speech?

Men drink kwete beer,
Women cook goat meat
And make millet bread,
But I am not there
To distribute the dishes
Among the elders!
The priests throw morsels
Of chicken meat,
They squirt goat blood
And poor libations
To the assembled ghosts
Of the dead,
But how can I address

The ghosts of my fathers
From here?

How can they put chymes
On my chest and back?
How can my grandmother
Spit blessing on me?

My age-mates have donned
White ostrich feathers,
They are singing a war song,
I want to join them
In the wilderness
And chase Death away
From our village,
Drive him a thousand miles
Beyond the mountains
In the west,
Let him sink down
With the setting sun
And never rise again.

I want to join
The funeral dancers,
I want to tread the earth
With a vengeance
And shake the bones
Of my father in his grave!

14

oasis

Listen to the sandy tunes
Of the desert song
As it rides the sand dunes
Accompanied by the winds
Singing through the palm leaves,
I want to hold hands
With the Arabs
And dance together
With the Israelis,

We shall dance
By an oasis
And cool our feet and hearts
With the water
Of the oasis!

I want to dance the rumba
And the cha cha cha,
I want to dance the white dances
Of the west
And shuffle my feet
Softly on the polished
And powdered wooden floor,
I want to dance
The dances of yellow men
At sunset....
Show me the sword dance
Of the Russians, and the beer songs
Of Germany!
And I will dance,
I will dance the bamboo
Dance of the Chinese
And the rice dance
Of the Japanese,
I will dance with the
Garlanded Vietnamese girls
In the swamps....

     *   *   *

You deaf Brother
Standing there with a club
In your hand,
Can you not read
My sign language?

Cut off this rope,
Open the steel gate,
I want to dance the dances
Of colonialists and communists,
I want to try the dances,
Of neo-colonialists and ex-Nazis
I want to dance the dances
Of our friends and
The dances of our enemies,
I want to lift their daughters
To my shoulder
And elope with them ....
          *   *   *
Let the Eskimo play and sing
His snowy song
And I will dance
To its whaley rhythm,
Let the Spanish girls
Snap their song
With their fingers
And I will dance like a cock
Wooing a hen.

Let the Zulu girls
Click their mountain song
With their sweet tongues
And I will join the men,
We will strike the earth
Like the falling meteorite!

Listen to the wailing tune
Of the Indian song,
Listen to the purring drums,
I will touch the earth lightly
Like a butterfly
And twist my limbs
To the piercing rhythm
Of the lyre.

I want to hold
The delicate waist
Of the untouchable goddess
In sari,
I want to touch
The vibrating buttocks
Of the Muganda girl
Dancing the **nankasa**.

Let me strike the beaded navel
Of the **dingidingi** dancer....
Let me dance

And forget my sorrow,
Let me forget
That I am jobless
And landless,
Forget that I am hopeless
And helpless,
Let me sweat out my frustrations
And anger.

Who wants to know
That his children
Will never go to school
Will never get a job
Or land
Or cow
Or goat!
Or chicken?
Let me dance
And forget!

I want to dance
All the dances of the world,
I want to sleep with
All the young dancers . . . .
Let me dance and forget . . . .

15

undergrowth

Who are playing
At the night club
Tonight?

* * *

The Blacks of America
Pour their souls
Over the Water,

Who can resist

The haughty twangs
Of your guitar
And the fat jabs
On the black piano?

Blast the metal horns,
Suck the sexyphones
With your fat lips,
Let me dance to the cutting throbs
Of your wounded song. . . .

*   *   *

Listen to the orphans
Wailing in the Nigerian
High-life tune,
Listen to the bombs
Bursting in the market place
Scattering the neat heaps of yams
And pieces of human bones,
I hear the food planes
Exploding in mid air,
The ash of the food
Falls gently on the heads
Of starving children. . . .
Listen to the clash of bayonets
As brother digs into brother's chest,
Listen to the beautiful chorus
Of the patriots,

**The only good Black
Is a dead one!**

*   *   *

Who are playing
At the night club
Tonight?

The Congo forest
Is on fire,
Listen to the groans
Of the elephants
Vomiting water on their
Burning backs,
Listen to the giraffes and pigs
The hippopotami tear
Through the forest climbers
And undergrowths.

Listen to the hunting drums
And the hunting horns
Mingling with the howls
Of hunting dogs,
See the river of pain
On the face of the singer,
The anguish of rape
Bloodshed and death. . . .

Black corpses strewn

Along the streets,
Dead to free Africa
So that they may
Suffer in
Freedom!

A white mercenary
Falling with a spear
Through his liver,
Dying to save Africans
From Africans.
A white nun
Her face white
As death,
Four more Black heroes
Waiting their turn....

Sing Brother,
Sing,
Cover me with the bile
From your heart,
Pump it out with
Your powerful lungs,
I want to bathe in it
And mix it with mine!

*   *   *

Free my hands and feet
You uniformed Stone,

Open the steel gate,
I want to join the dances
Of the world,
I want to shake my madness
Off my head,
I want to forgive
And forget the past,
I want to forget
As you have, conveniently, forgotten
That I was your body-guard,
That I organised your meetings
And shouted your slogans. . . .
I want to forget the scar
On my left arm
Which stopped the club
From squashing your skull,
Let me dance vigorously
And laugh at myself,
Let me forget that
I used to get you girls. . . .

       *   *   *

Open the door,

Man,
I want to dance
All the dances of the world,
I want to sleep with
All the young dancers.

I want to dance
And forget my smallness,
Let me dance and forget
For a small while
That I am a wretch,
The reject of my Country,
A broken branch of a Tree
Torn down by the whirlwind
Of Uhuru.

song of malaya

contents

Sister Prostitutes
Wherever you are

I salute you

Wealth and Health
To us all

Karibu *Come in
Enter* . . . .

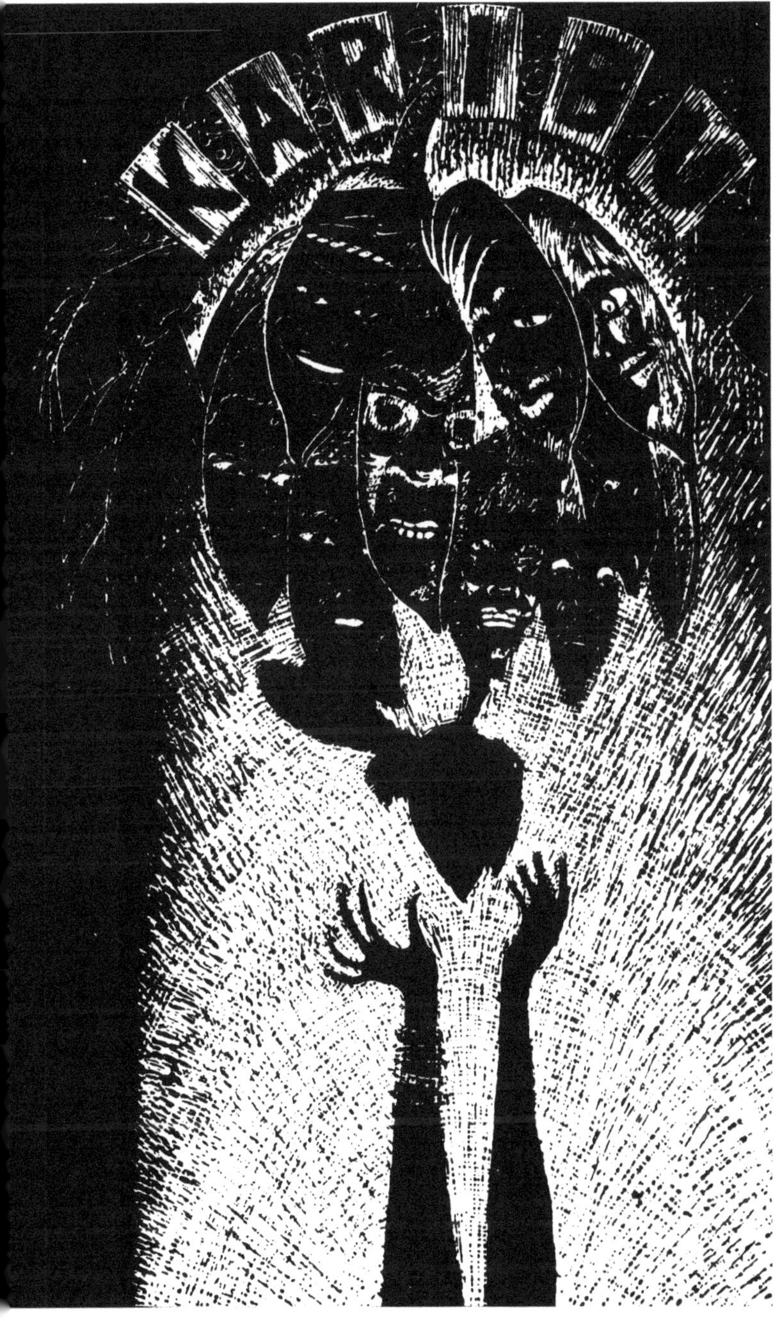

1

karibu

Welcome ashore
You vigorous young sailor,
I see you scanning the horizon
In search of dry land

I hear your heart drumming
Tum-tum-tu-tu-tum . . .

That time bomb
Pulsating in your loin

Surely weighs you down!
Oh...oh!

You soldier
Home bound,
I hear your song ....
I see the girls
On the platform
Waving a farewell ....

You reprieved murderer
You prisoner and detainee
About to be released,
Your granaries full
To overflow ....

Welcome home!

You drunken Sikhs
The night club
Your battle ground,
Turbans, broken heads
And broken glass
Strewn on the floor ....

Are your wives here?

And you skinny

Indian vegetarian
Your wife breeding
Like a rat,
Welcome to my table too,
I have cooked red meat
With spices . . . .
You hairy
Thick-skinned white miner
At Kilembe, at Kitwe . . . .

You sweating engineer
Building roads and bridges,
I see the cloud of dust
Raised by your bumping Land Rover
Heading for the City.

Karibu, Come in,
Enter . . . .

All my thanks
To you
Schoolboy lover,
I charge you
No fee . . . .

That shy smile
On your face,
And . . . .

Oh!
I feel ten years
Younger . . . .

Hey! Listen . . . .
Do not let the
Teacher know . . . .
Mm . . . mmm?
He was here
Last night . . . !

    *   *   *

Welcome you teachers
Teaching in bush schools,
I see you in buses
And on bicycles
Coming into the City
Your trouser pockets
Bulging with wallets . . . .

    *   *   *

Chieftain,
I see your gold watch
Glittering on your wrist,
You are holding
Your wife's waist
And kissing her
Good-bye.

Your shimmering briefcase

Is pregnant . . . .

How long
Will your Conference last?
You bus drivers
And you taxi men
Driving away from your home towns,
Will you be back
Tonight?

*   *   *

You factory workers
Do you not hear
The bells?
Is that not the end
Of your shift?

You shop assistants
Standing there all day
Displaying your wares
And persuading the customers
With false smiles

When do you close?

*   *   *

Brother,
You leader of the People,
How is our Party doing?
How many rallies

Have you addressed today?
How many hands
Have you shaken?

Oh — oh...
Your blue shirt
Is dripping wet with sweat,
Your voice is hoarse,
You look a bit tired
Friend ....

I have cold beer
In the house,
I have hot water
And cold water,
You must rest
A little,
Drink and eat
Something ....

Brother,
Come!

* * *

Sister Harlots
Wherever you are,
Wake up
Wash up

Brighten up,
Go gay and clean,
Lay
Your tables
Bring in fresh flowers . . . .

Load your trays
With fresh fruits
Fresh vegetables
And plenty of fresh meat . . . .
The hungry lions
Of the World
Are prowling around. . .
Hunting!

2

rich harvest

But you
Big Chief,

Why do you look at me
As if I were a bunch
Of hornets?
Why do you hiss
Like a frightened cobra
And bark at me

As if I were
A thief?

  ＊ ＊ ＊

Why, Baba...
Was it not you
Three nights ago?
Or was it four nights ago?

Do you not remember
Bursting into my house
Forcing me down
And tearing my knickers . . .
As if I were unwilling...?

  ＊ ＊ ＊

Oh-ha-ya-ya!
But you were drunk,
You could not finish . . . .
You feigned sleep,
Snoring like a pregnant hippo . . . .

Your silly baby tortoise
Withdrew its shrunken skinny neck...
Leaving me on fire
The whole night long . . .!

  ＊ ＊ ＊

But did I not take care
Of you in my house

And woke you up
Before the cock
Knocked on the door of Day?
And you were grateful,
You smiled and wished me
G o o d   D a y !
And promised to meet me
That evening . . . .
Don't you remember . . .?

    *   *   *

And, Chief,
How do you know
It was I
Who gave IT to you, anyway?

Did I not see you
Disappear behind the
Night Club
With my friend Achola?

    *   *   *

Did the Moon
Tell a lie
When it shone
On you two,
Arms and thighs intertwined
Like forest climbers,
Like pythons strangling

Their victims...?

We all heard Achola's
Song of joy,
          Mama-Mama-Mama...
          Brother, you are killing ....

Did you not hear
The grass and the dry leaves
Humming the chorus?

Her young breasts
Sunk deep into your chest
Hurting your bursting heart,
You threw heated stones
Into her cave
And broke all her ribs...
And when you rose
The yellow seeds of sweat
On your face
And the spark of joy,
Dancing on your trembling lips
Hid the grief, shame and fear
In your half closed eyes ....

For
Whose harvest is richer
Than Achola's?

*   *   *

Tell me you Men
Who split open
The **opok** tree
And scoop out the honey
With your bare hands,
Fearing not the bees . . .

Do you take
Some of the honey
To your wives?

Do they also
Enjoy the sweet fruits
Of your adventures?

*   *   *

Doctor,
I see you stabbing
The Chief's buttocks
With the poisoned arrow,
My Sister is wriggling
As you have orgasm
And pour bottled sperm
Into her flesh . . .
Tut-tut-tut-tut . . . .

*   *   *

Tell me
You mayors and town clerks,

When will you destroy
The stinging weeds
From the City Parks?

And you headmistresses
And headmasters . . .
Where are your gardeners?
Do you not see
The wild thorn trees
Blossoming in your compounds?
You Presidents, Ministers,
Liberators of Africa,
You heroes,
You who defeated colonialism
And imperialism,
True sons of Africa
Brave fighters against
Corruption and decay,
You revolutionaries . . .

Where are the advisors
The experts and mercenaries?

Can we not free Africa
From this one pest?

*   *   *

Ho-ho-ho . . .
But, **Bwana**

You are not so shy,
Are you?
Why don't you
Just ring up
Your doctor friend
And tell him
That you and your wife
Have **tonsilitis**. . .?

Okay?

     *   *   *

And why don't you
Get circumcised
You Kaffir?

Do you not know
That your leather bag
Carries the insects?

And bring your
Gum boots
For trudging in
The muddy field. . .

Okay. . .?

     *   *   *

Sister Whores
Wherever you are,
Come out,

Out into the open World,
The air is cool
And filled with bird song,
The Solomons are singing
In the rose gardens
And the flutes of the frogs
Mingle with the honks
Of hunting car-men . . .

                *   *   *

But, hey!
Listen,
The boxing gloves . . .
Carry the gloves
In your handbags . . . .

Sister Prostitutes
Wherever you are,
Wealth and health
To us all.

Come on, Sister,
Do you think
Your wild screams
And childish sobs
Are sweet music
In the ears of
Our man?

3

part-time

And you
My married Sister,
You whose husband
I also love dearly,

When will you learn
To be grateful
To me?

     *   *   *

When you turn
Into a bloody bitch
And he storms out
Of your house,
Mad at you, hungry, thirsty...

Is it not I
Who give our man
Water to wash his face
And to bathe?

Is it not I
Who nurse and soothe him
Like my own baby?

Does he not return to you
Clean shaven, smiling
Like a boy of fifteen
Does he ever come home
With a dirty shirt...?

*   *   *

Ho-ho-ho-ho...

Your eyes are black
With jealousy,
The veins of your neck
Are bursting with boiling blood.

Biting her lips,
Who is that brute

Her fists clenched,
Tears streaming down her cheeks?
She is stumping the wooden floor
And banging the table
Like a mad thing . . . .

Ha-ya-ya-ya-yaaah!

Come on, Sister,
Do you think
Your wild screams
And childish sobs
Are sweet music
In the ears of
Our man?

*   *   *

Sister,
What did your mother
Teach you?
To welcome your man
With lips locked by anger?

But your teeth
Are beautiful and white,
Do you not clean your mouth
In the morning?
Do you fear that

You might drive your man out
With the stench
Of your mouth?

    *   *   *

My friend,
Did your father teach you
To hate your husband's
Outside wives?
To hate his children
By his part-time wives?

    *   *   *

You have two little daughters,
I have **three** sons . . . .
Our husband is father
To, at least, five kids . . . .

So . . . .

    *   *   *

I am an open **pollok** blossom,
Bees, butterflies, moths . . .
Visit me by day and by night,
Except when the moon
Has appeared, and the dam
Of the Red River is broken . . .
Or when my cave
Is celebrating the visit
Of a newcomer . . . .

    *   *   *

A busy woman
Cannot tell the archer
That has scored the bull's eye,
But is it difficult
To convince another bull
That the seed in the gourd
Is his?

What better proof
Of manhood?
Especially when the wife
In the house
Eats lizard eggs
To prevent pregnancy!

*   *   *

But tell me, Sister,
Do you think
There is something wrong
With your husband
That he need
Have only one woman
For the rest of his life?

Do you not feed him well?

Do you think he is
Getting too fat?
Does he not get

Enough exercise?

Has the doctor told him
That he has a heart disease,
And ordered him to sleep with
Only one woman
For the rest of his life?

     *   *   *

But I find him
All right!
He comes to me
Ah!
Like a buffalo youth . . . .
I love your man
Truly!

Sister Prostitutes
Wherever you are,
Listen to the call
Loud . . . clear.

     *   *   *

Tear off that sleep
Glued to your body
Like a tick,
Break off his kisses
That seal your eyes.

Come Sister,

Quick ...
The World is drowning
In flames ....

     *   *   *

The mechanic handling metals
All day, hands cut,
Bleeding black oil ...

The farmer carting vegetables
For tomorrow's
Market Day...

The middle-aged Chieftain
His shrunken feet
Of his boyhood days ...
Too small for the sandals

Black students
Arriving in Rome,
In London, in New York...
Arrows ready, bows drawn
For the first white kill ....

     *   *   *

Listen to the ocean liner
Crying in labour pain
As she approaches the harbour...
Steel hawks
Shitting at airports ...

The bus . . .

Trains' bellies
Bursting at the stations . . .
Do you see
The maggots
Limping from the wounds
Of loneliness?
They crawl in haste
To the motherly warmth
Of your embrace . . .

    *   *   *

Angel Prostitutes
Wherever you are
Come now, now . . .
Bear these wretches
Into your heaven!

Put forward those shapely legs
Smooth like elephant tusks
Powerful like pythons . . . .

Pull away the curtains
Covering your dancing waists
And mighty hips,
Sweep away the clouds
That sit in the valley
Between the mountains
Of your breasts . . . .

*   *   *

Walk softly like a cat
My Sister,
But ready to wield
The deadliest stroke
With your smile . . . .

The open simple smile
For the egg-headed scholars,
The hot devil smile
For the priests and their kind,
The cool confident smile
For the faint-hearted and the unsure,
The innocent infant smile
For the fatherly and the senile,
The pious shy smile
For the thieves and the diseased,
The poverty-stricken **smile**
For the pot-bellied rich,
The haughty deceitful smile
For the politicians and robbers.
The girlish foolish smile
For the schoolboy
And the middle-aged nit-wit,
The frozen secret smile
For the dark-suited simpleton,
The quick winged smile

The open simple smile
For the egg-headed scholars,
The hot devil smile
For the priests and their kind,
The cool confident smile
For the faint-hearted and the unsure . . .

For the Chief's messengers and reporters,
The fearful savage smile
For the poor white bastards,
The monkey town smile
For the opportunist get-rich-quick . . . .
       *   *   *
Hold your head high,
My Sister,
The entire arena of the night
Is yours . . . .

Our cowardly competitors
Have run away,
Are hiding behind
Those drawn curtains
Biting their nails,
The bitter smoke of jealousy
In their eyes. . .
Tears . . . .
       *   *   *
Oh-oh-oh-oh. . .
Sister. . .
Take your rightful share
Of your man . . . .

Take him by the hand
Along the beautiful garden
Along the Red River,

Let him play with the soft grass
And touch the slippery banks . . . .

Give him a ride
On the mad mule,
Up and down
The steep hillside . . . .

Let him taste
The wild honey
He cannot get
In his own home . . . .

       *   *   *

Sister **Malayas**
Wherever you are,
Wealth and health
To us all.

4

take the sickle

You black Bishop
Preaching morality . . .

But your father
Had six wives,
Your mother
Was not one of them,
Was she?

What weak-kneed morality

You talk!
     *   *   *
Do you actually pray
To God
To bless each bee
So that it should
Stick to one flower?

And each butterfly
And each moth
And each male ladybird,
Should it visit only one flower
In its life-time?

Would you take your sickle
And slash the flowers
In your garden
To ensure that the remainder
Have but one visitor
Each?
     *   *   *
Would you condemn
Other men's daughters
To a sexless life
Like nuns,
But against their will?

And my grandfather

162

Will he burn
In the fire below
For loving ten women
And looking after their children,
While you go to the place above
Because you did not
Make love to a woman?

And for the unmarried
Like myself,
Would you have me
Block up the mouth
Of my cave?

Would you cut a man's throat
To save him
From thirst?

*   *   *

Listen, Sister Prostitutes

In the Hilton suites,
And you at the Apolo
And at the Acholi Inn. . . .

Fill your glasses
With champagne . . .

And you in the slums
Distilling illegal gin,

Here's to Eve
With her golden apple ....
We'll drink to the
Daughters of Sodom
And to the daughters of Gomorrah ....

And you brewing millet beer . . . .

Take some drink
In the half gourd . . . .
Raise your glasses and half gourds
My Sisters,
And click them with mine . . . .
Here's to Eve
With her golden apples,
And to the Egyptian girl
Who stole Abraham
From Sarah's bed . . . .

We'll drink to the
Daughters of Sodom
And to the daughters of Gomorrah
Who set the towns ablaze
With their flaming kisses . . . .

Let's drink to Rahab
With her two spy boy friends,
To Esther the daughter of Abigail,
To Delilah and her bushy-headed
Jaw bone gangster,
To Magdalena who anointed
The feet of Jesus!

We will remember Theodora
The Queen of Whores

Who struck Chief Justinian's marriage
With her embrace
And flung his wife
Beyond the deserts,
And the unknown Prostitute Sister
Who fired Saint Augustine
To the clouds . . . .

  · *   *   *

Sister Prostitutes
Wherever you are,
Power and fame
To us all!

5

peals of crying

My sweet baby,
Mm!
You tickle my teats
With your toothless kisses
And remind me
Of my first love . . . .

I was thirteen
Or may be fourteen . . . .

      *   *   *

Mm!
How sweet you are
My darling,
I love you,
Oh!
I love . . . .

    *   *   *

But . . .
You have stopped smiling?
Why do you want
To cry?

Are you tired?
Sleepy?
Is this the cry
That comes
Before sleep?

Are you ill
My love?

Or are you missing
A father?

    *   *   *

Come
My darling,
Stop stabbing your
Mum's heart

With the peals
Of your crying . . . .

I am
Deadly lonely,
My love . . . .

       *   ✻   ✻

And . . .
Who is that sobbing?

What is it
My boy . . .?

Are you hungry?
Ah-ahaaa!
But do you know
What Mum has cooked
For you?

       *   *   *

What?

Someone at school
Called you
A b a s t a r d . . .
I l l e g i t . . .?

Is that all?
Tut-tut-tut-tut . . . .

Is that why
You cry?

Come here
My Boy,
Come and sit
On my lap . . . .

Now,
Tell me.

Who was the greatest Man
That ever lived?

The Saviour
Redeemer
The Light . . .
King of Kings
The Prince of Peace . . .
My big Boy.

Tell Mommy.

What was His Father's name?

Was the Carpenter
Really His father?
            *   *   *

Stop crying

172

My love,
Dry up your tears, Son,
Have some fish
Here's some porridge,
With *ugali* . . . .

*   *   *

And you bush teacher
Troubling my son,
How dare you
Throw the first stone
While Christ writes
In the sand?

*   *   *

How many teen-agers
Have you clubbed
With your large headed hammer,
Sowing death in their
Innocent fields?
Who does not know
The little girls
In your class
Who are your wives,
And the children
That these children
Have
By you?

*   *   *

Sister Harlots
Wherever you are,
The bedcovers of the World
Have been removed . . . .

Wives, house boys,
Hotel slaves . . .
Have made the beds . . .
Fresh . . . no crumpled pillows . . .
The carpets, sofas,
Car seats, Park benches . . . .

The winds have spread
Cushions of freshly fallen leaves
In the fields,
The lawns in the City Parks
Are trimmed . . . .
        *   *   *
Sister Prostitutes
Wherever you are
Victory and health
To us all!

6

the duet

And you Brother
Son of my mother . . . .

You no longer speak with me,
And when our eyes meet
They are quickly averted,
It may be with hate
Or maybe
With shame?

I see you spitting
With contempt,
I hear you muttering
That I have brought disgrace
On the family . . . .

They tell me
That you have threatened
To shoot me
If I come to your house
Because I might
Contaminate you
And your children,
And teach your wife
Bad ways . . . .

       *   *   *

A-haaa!

Tell me
Son of my mother,
Tell me,
Where were you
Two nights ago,
Soon after the bars
Where closed?

Do you remember
The number of your room?

Of course,
You did not know
That I
Was in the next room
With your friend,
Your boss...

Yaaaah!
*   *   *

And, my God!
The noises you made....!

The soft drumming on the
Dancing mattress,
The bedstead gritting
Her teeth,
The duet ....

And why were you
Shouting our mother's name?
What did you want
Her to come there for?

The whole Lodge
Was awakened ....
*   *   *

Brother
Tell me about

Your beautiful Queen,
Faithful?
Innocent?
Sweet?
Yes?

*   *   *

And when you go
On safari
Or to the office . . .

When she goes
To the market
Or to buy things
From the medicine shop,
Or to do her hair. . .

On Sundays
When she goes for the Mass
Or to the Confession. . .

Brother,
Do you lock up
The gate of her Palace
And keep the Key
With you?

*   *   *

Have you not yet discovered
That quite often

The foresters come
To your hunting ground,
Fell your tall **mvuli tree**
And split it down the middle
In your own garden?

*   *   *

And the hunters,
Do they not
Chop up their victim
In your own kitchen,
And use the towel
In your bathroom
To wipe the blood
Off their spears and knives?

Look at the slaves
Of the World
Calling themselves
Wives,
Penned like goats
To unwilling pegs....

Married whores of the World
Why don't you
Leave me alone?

And you
Bastard son of my father,

I have not come to you
For help,
My children are healthy
And happy,
They do not go about
In tattered clothes,
Dirty, untrimmed . . . .

Why don't you
Just shut up . . .?

But if you like
I can help you,
I can find you
A sweet. . . .

7

flaming eternity

You Sergeant
Arresting me now,
Sir,
But we were together
In my house
Only last night . . .!
And . . . oh-oh-oh . . .!

And after cutting . . .

Axing with your blunt battle-axe . .
And smearing the wound
With ghee . . .

You just walked out . . .

Without even . . .
You know . . . .

But how can you now
Call me
A vagrant?

        *   *   *
Let the disappointed men
Shout abuses at us,
Let them groan, sleepless,
Their spears vomiting butter,
Their buttocks swollen
After the doctor's caning . . . .

        *   *   *
Let their jealous wives
Rage and beat them
With beer bottles
And stab them with knives . . . .

        *   *   *
Let the bitches
Pour boiling water on us
And drop boiling oil

Into our ears . . . .

Let them fight us
In the night clubs
And tear our new dresses,
Gifts from their husbands . . . .
        *   *   *
Let their secret
Schoolgirl wives hiss
And swear at us
In whispers . . . .
        *   *   *
Let our parents
Spit curses,
Let our brothers
Choke with shame and anger
And run mad . . . .
        *   *   *
Let the black Bishops
And priests
Preach against us,
Let them sow their seeds
In snow white fields
As they pray
To Saint Peter
Not to allow us
Through Heaven's Gate . . . .
Let the Lord

Grant their prayers
And condemn us all
To flaming eternity . . . .
*   *   *
Let Parliamentarians
Debate and pass laws
Against us,
Let the police arrest us
And lock us up
In their cells,
Let the magistrates
Sentence us to jails . . .
*   *   *
But
Who can command
The sun
Not to rise in the morning?

Or having risen
Can hold it
At noon
And stop it
From going down
In the west?
*   *   *
Sister prostitutes
Wherever you are
Wealth and health
To us all . . . .